STO J

FRIENDS
OF ACPL

W9-CVA-887

jE
Clarke, Gus.
Scratch 'n' sniff

MAY 2 6 1999

ALLEN COUNTY PUBLIC LIBRARY
FORT WAYNE, INDIANA 46802

You may return this book to any agency or branch
of the Allen County Public Library

DEMCO

Scratch 'n' Sniff

GUS CLARKE

ANDERSEN PRESS · LONDON

For Taufiq

Allen County Public Library
900 Webster Street
PO Box 2270
Fort Wayne, IN 46801-2270

Copyright © 1996 by Gus Clarke
The rights of Gus Clarke to be identified as the author and illustrator of this work have
been asserted by him in accordance with the Copyright, Designs and Patents Act, 1988.

First published in Great Britain in 1996 by Andersen Press Ltd., 20 Vauxhall Bridge Road,
London SW1V 2SA. This paperback edition first published in 1998 by Andersen Press Ltd.
Published in Australia by Random House Australia Pty., 20 Alfred Street,
Milsons Point, Sydney, NSW 2061. All rights reserved. Colour separated in Italy by
Fotoriproduzioni Grafiche, Verona. Printed and bound in Italy by Grafiche AZ, Verona.

10   9   8   7   6   5   4   3   2   1

British Library Cataloguing in Publication Data available.

ISBN 0 86264 810 6
This book has been printed on acid-free paper

"Where is it?   In here?   Or here?

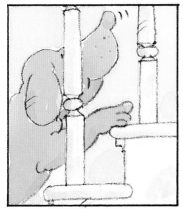 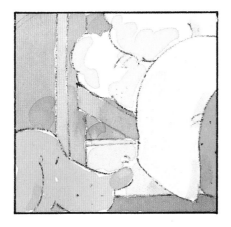 

Up here?   Under there?   Or over here?

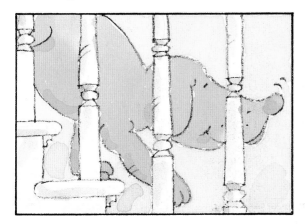 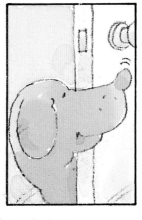 

Perhaps it *is* down here.   No.   So where is it?"

"Hello, Sniff," said Scratch. "What are you doing?"

"It's that smell again," said Sniff. "I don't know what it is, but it's very nice. I could smell it when I woke up this morning and I've been all round the house, but I can't find out where it's coming from."

"Perhaps it's coming from outside," said Scratch. "Why don't you go and have a look? It might be fish."

"I think you're right," said Sniff. "It does seem to be coming from outside. But it's not fish.

I'll just pop out and track it down. Will you be all right here on your own? You will behave yourself, won't you?"

"Of course," said Scratch. "I'll be fine. Now off you go and find that smell. There's no need to hurry back."

"Byeee!"

"Now, where is it?
Ah, yes. Over there.

Or is it over there?

This way?

No. It's definitely…er…that way. I think."

"Hello, Sniff," said Bernard. "Whad are you doig?"

"I'm looking for that nice smell," said Sniff. "Do you know where it's coming from?"

"Sorry, Sniff. Id's no good askig me. I dink I'm comig down wid a really bad code. Whad's id smell like?"

"Difficult to say," said Sniff. "It's a bit sort of sausagey. With strawberries… and ice cream…and some of those nice curly whirly pink and white sweeties."

"Sounds nice," said Bernard. "Save some for me if you find id. Bud now I'm goig home do bed. Good luck, Sniff."

"Thanks, Bernard," said Sniff. "Get better soon."

"Hello, Scruff," said Sniff. "Can you smell that lovely smell?"

"Yes," said Scruff. "Isn't it yummy!"

"It certainly is. Absolutely delicious," said Sniff.

"Which bit do you like best?" said Scruff.

"I'm not sure," said Sniff. "There's such a mixture. It might be the apple pie and custardy sort of smell, or the candyfloss, or the smoky bacony crispy smell. I can't really say. Which bit do *you* like best?"

"Well, I can't smell any of that," said Scruff. "I thought you meant the dustbins."

"Goodbye, Scruff," said Sniff.

"Good morning, Sebastian," said Sniff. "Have you noticed that rather nice smell?"

"Can you smell it where you are?" said Sebastian.

"Yes," said Sniff.

"Then it's most unlikely," said Sebastian. "I've never actually put my nose quite that close to the ground. What does it smell like?"

"Well," said Sniff, "let me think. It's a bit like burgers with lots and lots of ketchup. And chips. And a very large banana milkshake."

"And can you smell all that sort of thing down where you are?" said Sebastian.

"Yes," said Sniff.

"Ugh!" said Sebastian. "In that case I'm really rather glad to be up here."

"Sorry to bother you," said Sniff.

"'Ello, Sniff," said Spike. "Wassamatta? Bad smell or suffink? 'S not me."

"No," said Sniff. "It's a nice one. Can't you smell it?"

"Not wiv me nose," said Spike. "Wass it of?"

"Well, you know those nice thin minty chocolates that melt in the mouth?" said Sniff. "And there's peachy yoghurt. And some of those little cheesy biscuits."

"Any leg in it?" said Spike. "I like a bit of leg now and again."

"Sorry, Spike," said Sniff. "It's not really your sort of smell, is it?"

"Nah," said Spike. "I gotta go. I wanna catch the postman."

"Hello, Sniff," said Fifi. "What do you think of my new perfume?"

"It's very…er…strong," said Sniff.

"Yes, isn't it lovely," said Fifi. "What are you doing?"

"I've been trying to find a nice smell."

"What's it like?"

"Well, it's sort of…
gone now. All I can
smell is you, Fifi."

"Oh, Sniff. What a
lovely thing to say,"
said Fifi.

"I really must be getting
home now, Fifi," said Sniff.
"I left Scratch all on his
own. I hope he's not been
too lonely and bored."

"Come on, you lot. It's time to go," said Scratch.
"Help me clear up before Sniff gets back."

"Goodbye, boys," said Scratch. "See you tomorrow. Same time. Don't forget to bring the water pistols!"

"Are you sure Sniff will be going out again? You know how fussy he can be."

"Don't worry," said Scratch. "I'm sure."

"Hello, Sniff. How did it go? Any luck?"

"No," said Sniff. "I couldn't find it anywhere. And no one else could smell it at all."

"Never mind," said Scratch. "Come on in. It's nearly bedtime. I've had such a quiet day without you."

"Night night, Sniff," said Scratch. "Sleep tight."

"You too," said Sniff.

But later that
night...

"Shhh!"

Plip!

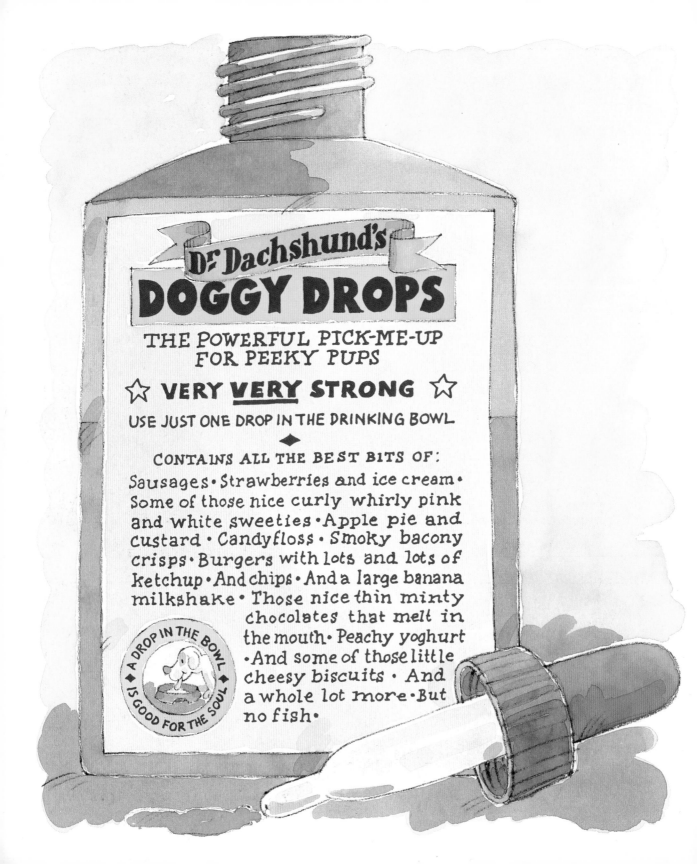

"It is!

It's there again.

Mmmmm!

I wonder where it is…"